29

L M Thornwood

Copyright © 2024 by L M Thornwood

All rights reserved.

No portion of this book may be reproduced in any form without written permission from the publisher or author, except as permitted by U.S. copyright law.

CONTENTS

CHAPTER ONE 6

CHAPTER 2 15

CHAPTER 3 24

CHAPTER 4 28

CHAPTER 5 35

CHAPTER 6 45

CHAPTER 7 50

CHAPTER 8 57

CHAPTER 9 65

CHAPTER 10 73

CHAPTER 11 80

CHAPTER 12 86

CHAPTER 13 89

CHAPTER 14 93

CHAPTER 15 98

CHAPTER 16 102

EPILOGUE 107

The 29.5-day cycle originates from the lunar cycle, which is the period it takes the Moon to complete its phases from new moon to new moon. This cycle is known as a synodic month and averages about 29.5 days.

Chapter One

October 25, 2024, 8:15pm EST

Snowflakes whipped across my face as I lay on my back, staring up into the storm. The cold felt distant, numbed by a dull ache spreading through my body. I tried to breathe, but each breath was harder than the last, and I couldn't remember why.

I must have slipped. Maybe I hit my head. I could see the open door of a nearby vehicle, its interior light casting an eerie glow onto the snow. That must be it—I fell, got disoriented.

But then, through the fog clouding my mind, a shadow moved into view. A man in black, holding something that looked like a pistol. And just like that, clarity hit me like a slap to the face.

He was the killer. The man I'd been hunting for years. And now, I was about to become his final victim.

I had failed. Failed to stop him, failed my sister, and failed all the women he'd taken before me.

October 25, 2024, 6:15 pm EST

I had been driving for hours, and I had the window open just enough to let the cold air blow in. It was the only thing keeping me awake at the moment. I had to get to a small town in Virginia because in two days' time, there was going to be a murder—and not just one, but several.

Flashing lights ahead forced me to slow down even more on the highway. The snow was coming down heavier, and the road was definitely white. A truck I'd been following had come to a stop, and a police vehicle was blocking the other lane. I had no option to go around.

When the truck pulled away, I watched it slowly proceed down an exit ramp. The officer was motioning me forward, and I complied.

"Sorry, miss, but we had to shut the highway down. Best guess is it won't be open until sometime in the morning."

The man was young, definitely in his twenties, and he wasn't a regular cop; he was wearing a deputy sheriff's uniform and badge. I couldn't see his hair through the cap he wore, but his blue eyes were light and vibrant in a way I hadn't noticed on many men before.

"Miss, did you hear me about pulling off the ramp?"

Had I really not heard what he said? "Sorry," I replied, looking away from him. "I'm going."

The man placed his hand on my lowered window. "Are you okay, miss?"

What a loaded question, I thought. I stuck with a simple answer. Turning my head to look at him again, I saw those eyes lock with mine. There was concern and compassion there, and I so wanted someone to talk to about what I was doing and what had happened to me. But this wasn't the time or place. "I'm good, just tired," I said.

He nodded, and I pulled away down the ramp I'd seen the truck take. At the bottom, I had only the choice to go to the right, as large road-closed signs blocked the way to the left.

Fortunately, there was an all-night gas station nearby, and I could see a motel on top of the hill. Sleep sounded good, but the images of Kelly and Susan kept flashing into my mind whenever I closed my eyes. I had never met either girl before, but I knew the killer's type: dark hair, blue eyes. Both had gone missing after visiting a bar with friends. I'd told the local authorities everything I knew, but in my opinion, they still weren't doing enough.

I slid into the parking lot, barely avoiding hitting another parked car. I kept it off to the side, rolled up my windows, pulled the pistol from my glove box, and tucked it neatly behind my back at the waistband before getting out. My jacket was in the back seat, so I retrieved it but didn't put it on.

The cold felt refreshing and kept me invigorated. I doubted I would run into any trouble here, but fate had a funny way of throwing things at you when you least expected it.

There were several doors: one for the diner, one that looked like it led to a hallway, and another for the gas station store. It was the most lit up and probably had the most accessible restroom.

I felt the pressure on my bladder and had to think back to when I'd last gone. The door slid open for me, and a blast of warm air hit my face as I stepped inside. The smell of hotdogs, nachos, and cheese wafted through the place, making my stomach gurgle at the thought of food.

It had probably been many hours since I'd eaten, but first things first. Take a whizz, as my younger brother used to call it, and then decide if I wanted cheap nachos or real food from the diner.

From the outside windows, the place had looked packed, and now I could smell bacon and eggs. The clerk ignored me as I walked by the counter and toward the hanging restroom sign.

The clerk was a young woman with black lipstick, black hair, and black nails. She had a couple of blue teardrop tattoos under her right eye, and I couldn't tell what kind of magazine she was reading.

It didn't matter if she ignored me. I preferred to operate unnoticed. There was something empowering about being unseen. It was like I was the predator watching my prey.

A hallway to the restrooms was tucked behind a row of coolers, housing beer and sodas. The floor was dirty, smeared with black footprints, and the women's bathroom was a complete disaster.

Two of the stalls had been taped off with yellow caution tape, and the third and final stall had a used condom that hadn't made its way into the toilet. At first, I thought about complaining to the clerk, but then reasoned that she wouldn't do anything about it, and by this point, I really had to go.

So, holding my breath, I used some toilet paper to

remove the condom. Then I used more paper and some hand sanitizer from a small bottle attached to my keys to wipe the toilet seat down.

It wasn't perfect or the most sanitary, but it gave me enough peace of mind to squat down on it. Afterwards, the smell of bacon overpowered my thoughts, and I headed straight for the diner. There was a hallway between the gas station and the diner. I had no idea where it led, but I could definitely hear the campy carnival-like music of claw games nearby, along with the tumbling sound of dryers. I guessed there was probably a laundromat for truckers around the bend.

I never understood why people wasted money on those claw games. They were rigged—I was certain of it. The diner was mostly booths with high backs, making it hard to see around, but once I reached a more central location, I could see men sitting at a bar close to the kitchen. Just about every booth was filled with men, and judging by the way they were dressed, they were all truckers. Ball caps and blue jeans on nearly every one of them.

I could feel every eye turn my way, and I didn't like it. I wanted to be unseen, so I quickly went to an empty booth and pulled out my phone. I'd discovered that most people will ignore you when you're on your phone, but it also gave me a way to observe others without drawing too much attention.

Like now, I was making mental notes of some of the clientele. The killer could be among them; he would likely be traveling this highway to get to the town. It was the most direct route, and some of what I knew about him was that he was fairly young, twenty-nine to thirty, and had to be attractive enough to lure the women he trapped. He came from money but probably didn't flaunt it.

I made this assumption because he never stayed in one state for long. On my big map of missing women, there were recent cases matching his type from several states.

A middle-aged waitress in a pink skirt approached the table and handed me a menu. She had dark bags under her eyes and a wrist brace on her right hand. "The menu is kind of light tonight. We can do eggs, bacon, pancakes, hotdogs, and fries for now."

So there really was no point in her handing me a menu if those were my only choices. "Scrambled eggs and some bacon," I said without hesitation.

She gave me a faint smile, revealing yellow-stained teeth that matched the stains on her right thumb and forefinger. It was obvious that the woman was a heavy smoker.

Before my encounter with the twenty-nine-day killer, I would never have noticed little details like that. Hell, I have a hard time even imagining my life before. I often question if I really cared about anything. I know I cared for my family, but the trauma of their deaths was just a numb place in the back of my mind now.

I knew it hurt before. So why didn't I feel it now?

My thoughts were interrupted by the screams of several people as an out-of-control car came crashing through the parking lot, smashing into several parked vehicles before heading straight toward one of the diner's glass windows.

I was far enough away from the imploding glass to

avoid being hit, but others fled in all directions as the car's horn blared and emergency lights flickered.

While everyone else was panicking, I stood up and moved toward the wreckage. The cold and snow were blowing in, but that didn't bother me as I inched closer. There was a bald-headed man in the driver's seat, his head lying on the steering wheel, unmoving.

The window was shattered enough for me to step outside and approach the driver's door. Opening it, the bald man, dressed in nothing but his undergarments, toppled out toward me with his hand outstretched.

He'd been holding a revolver, which landed in the snow. He had obvious injuries; his white undershirt was soaked in crimson red and had several cut marks.

So, the injuries hadn't come from the car wreck. At first glance, it looked like he'd been stabbed multiple times in a fight somewhere. So where had he come from?

I reached out to feel for a pulse on the man's neck and found none, but there was something odd—a red abrasion on his wrists. I hadn't noticed it before, but now I was keenly aware of it. It was the mark of someone who had been tied down by a strap or belt. There was also a red welt along the main artery in his neck, right where I'd felt for a pulse.

This person, whoever he had been, was recently injected with something, and judging from my observations so far, it was not voluntary.

"Is he dead?" someone called out from the group of gawkers. Two men were pushing themselves through the broken windows and heading my way. I was surprised that the "boy scouts" of the group took this long to investigate, probably thinking I wasn't qualified to declare the man dead or not.

Sensing that my time was short to keep probing, I did a quick check of the other seat and found a manila folder with half of the contents scattered and the rest dumped onto the floorboard. One of the papers had a photograph of Kelly. There was no mistaking it.

A sticky note on the folder bore a motel name and room number. This man had either been staying at or visiting the Alpine Motel, which was just up the hill beside the station. A rather odd coincidence, but whoever this man was, he'd been looking for one of the girls I was also trying to find. He was either a hired PI or a detective looking into the case. I didn't think he was a family member of either girl, as I saw no discernible features that would suggest that. Of course, I could be wrong, but for now, I was content to consider him a private investigator.

Before I could reach in and take it, I was asked to step aside by two truckers who immediately began checking the body as if they could save his life—which they couldn't, since he was already dead. Most of the diner's patrons ventured out into the snow, and I simply slipped back inside, retrieving my jacket from the booth.

I put it on, found my white gloves in the pockets, and then returned to the gas station area. I still had questions about the dead man, and I doubted I'd find answers by staying with the body. The man was missing his pants, so the only place to look for clues was the Alpine Motel. And with the road conditions worsening, it would be safer for me to walk than to drive.

The goth clerk was no longer at the counter, and I glanced around to see if I could spot her, but there was no sign of that dark hair. Throwing my fur-lined hood up, I walked out into the storm with my hands in my pockets, determined to find out what the PI knew.

Chapter 2

The trek to the top of the hill was more treacherous than I'd anticipated. Several times, I almost slipped and would have fallen flat on my face, but I caught myself and proceeded cautiously.

A minute later, I reached the top. The motel was fully lit, and several cars were parked outside some of the rooms. A fairly fresh empty spot lay near the office, along with a trail of blood leading straight to the check-out office.

I paused, silently observing the scene while snow and ice chunks, whipped by the wind, smacked my face and bounced off my hood. There was no movement from the rooms or the office. Aside from the blood trail, the only thing that seemed out of place was a door to one of the nearby rooms—it was left ajar, possibly the room the PI had come from. Reaching behind my back, I pulled out my pistol and slipped it into my right-hand pocket.

I didn't feel like anyone was watching me, but my instincts told me to proceed with caution. So I stood there in the snow, just watching, for a couple of minutes before deciding to check out the office first.

Each step felt heavy as I walked around the crimson trail. I glanced back toward the motel rooms every now and then to make sure no one was approaching from that direction, but my main focus was on the door and desk ahead.

Beyond the counter, I saw something flickering. At first, I thought it might be a light, but as I stepped through the doorway into the warm room, I realized it was a TV show playing softly in the background.

More blood led me around the edge of the desk and through an open wooden panel. A few feet past the desk lay a bearded man, his chest stabbed multiple times. There were slash marks on his arms as well.

Just a foot or two away from the clerk was an open, blood-stained knife, likely the same weapon used on the dead man I'd found earlier in the car.

When had I become so cold and analytical? I wondered. Was I losing my sense of humanity in this hunt?

Taking a short breath to clear my thoughts, I began examining the back side of the desk. A bloody handprint revealed a holster taped to the underside of the desk, likely where the revolver had come from.

Another handprint was smeared on the inside of the desk, as if someone had grabbed something in a hurry—probably keys. So, why had the bald man stabbed the clerk to death and fled? Was it possible the clerk was involved in the kidnappings?

There had to be a connection. But was I really willing to disturb the crime scene in search of answers? I wasn't even sure what I should be looking for.

"Why don't I just go and check out the room with the

ajar door?" I muttered to myself. Sometimes, talking to myself helped bring clarity, and right now, I needed it more than ever.

After snapping a few photos with my phone, I backed out of the office and headed toward room three. The only cars parked near the motel were at the far end and the L-bend, with all the rooms closest to the office vacant.

Just as I reached the door, the lights flickered out, plunging me into darkness. The power lines must have failed, and with the storm raging on, I doubted they'd be fixed anytime soon.

Drawing out my pistol with one hand and turning on the light on my phone with the other, I pushed the door open, scanning the room from right to left. The bedroom was empty, but I checked the closet, the bathroom, and even under the bed to be sure.

My heart pounded as I examined the headboard. Thick leather straps were attached to it, snapped and broken from desperate thrashing. The rest of the restraints had been unbuckled. That explained how the man had escaped, but not who his captor was.

On the nightstand next to the bed were a couple of syringes and an unmarked vial with a clear liquid. Without a label, I wouldn't be able to identify it, so I left it untouched.

In one of the chairs near the TV were some clothes: a pair of black pants, a navy collared shirt, black socks, and loafers. In the back pocket was a billfold. Just as I was about to open it, I heard a sound outside the door.

A vehicle was approaching. There was no time to

escape, so I hid in the bathroom, pistol raised and ready.

Someone knocked on the door and announced themselves. "Hello, anyone inside? This is Deputy Dan Bluefield from the Grayson Sheriff's Department. I'm coming in."

Lowering my pistol, I stepped out of the bathroom with my hands up. "I'm the only one here," I said as the man flashed his light on me.

I couldn't tell if he had his pistol aimed at me, but his voice turned serious. "Miss, what are you doing here?"

"I walked up from the gas station to investigate where the dead man came from."

"Why would you do that? You should have stayed where it was safe."

Where to even start? "I'm looking for someone," I replied. "That man had her picture in his car."

"I saw it. Are you related to her?"

"No, but she was taken by a man who preys on young women who look like her." I recognized the voice as the same deputy who'd stopped me on the highway—his slight country drawl making it unique.

"If you're…" he began, but was cut off by nearby gunshots. He never lowered the light from my face. "Place your hands on top of your head," he ordered.

"Wait, you can't arrest me. I haven't done anything wrong."

"I found you in a crime scene, which is suspicious

enough to give me probable cause to detain you for questioning."

"That's ridiculous," I retorted. My mind screamed for me to run, but where would I go? There was a killer on the loose, and I could use this deputy's help to catch him.

"Now, place your hands on top of your head," he repeated.

This time, I complied, letting him cuff my hands behind my back. I expected him to be rough, but he was surprisingly gentle. Up close, I caught a faint, spicy scent from his cologne or body wash—pleasantly unexpected.

He patted down my pockets and found the pistol. My stomach clenched as he muttered to himself. "This is turning out to be one hell of a night. What's going on around here?"

After shoving me into the back seat of his SUV, I immediately felt for the fake scar patch on my wrist, beneath which I'd hidden a small piece of metal to pick locks. It was amazing what you could learn online.

The only problem was, I'd only practiced unlocking cuffs with my hands in front of me. This would be my first attempt with my hands behind my back. I mentally kicked myself for not practicing that.

Dan climbed into the front seat, glancing back at me with his blue eyes. "I'm sorry about this, miss, but I need to investigate the shooting. You'll be safe here."

Nowhere was safe—not with monsters like the twenty-nine-day killer walking free. I didn't say this, though; I was too focused on picking the lock. But I had questions for him. "Don't you have backup coming?"

Dan didn't look back, his attention focused on driving carefully down the hill in low gear. I'd seen chains on the tires, but they didn't stop the SUV from sliding here and there. The storm outside looked like it was only getting worse.

"Yes," he replied. "But the roads are so bad it'll take them a while to reach us."

"Look, I know you have questions for me. I'll give you the highlights so you understand what I'm doing here."

"Now's not the time, miss. There may be dead or injured people at the gas station, and I'm the closest person who can help them. Sit back and relax. I've got this."

Relax? I thought bitterly. "Dan, what I have to say is important. Whatever's happening here is the work of a very sick individual. I know because I was his only victim who survived."

He glanced at me in the rear-view mirror. "Are we talking about a serial killer?"

"Yes, the one they call the twenty-nine-day killer or the full moon slayer."

"I've heard of him—been at large for over a year. How do you know it's him?"

Memories of my sister's screams and the fire flooded my mind.

"Miss, how do you know it's him?"

I pushed the memories aside. "I've been hunting him.

The girl in the picture I told you about—she's his latest victim."

Dan's eyes flicked to the mirror again. "I don't want to doubt you, but that sounds hard to believe. How could you know?"

"He has a type: women aged eighteen to twenty, with dark hair and blue eyes."

"Alright. I'll be extra cautious," Dan said as he parked in front of the convenience store.

"Wait, don't you want more details about the killer?"

But Dan had already exited the vehicle, taking his shotgun with him. He left the SUV running, so heat still blasted through the vents, casting flickering light over the snow outside.

My fingers ached from trying to pick the lock. I should have practiced this position more. Finally, I saw a shape approaching from the front window and thought it was Dan—until the person climbed into the driver's seat.

It was definitely not Dan.

This person wore black from head to toe, including a ski mask and mirrored sunglasses. As he turned around,

he spoke.

"Jenifer, isn't it?"

Fear gripped me as I realized who this was. Thoughts of my own death raced through my mind. Would it be a quick gunshot or a drawn-out stabbing?

"The polite thing to do, Jenifer," he continued, his tone sharp, "is to answer my question."

Unable to speak, I nodded.

"I'm so glad we could finally meet. I have to say, you're my biggest fan. How long have you been tracking me?"

My mouth opened, but no words came out. All I could picture was my impending death.

"I see my presence has left you speechless," he sneered, "and I'm running out of time. Here's your one chance to ask me any question before I go."

The memory of my sister's murder surged to the forefront of my mind. Her screams, the fire, the monster leaping through the window.

"Why?" I managed to whisper.

He leaned closer to the grating separating us, his voice low and mocking. "Because, Jenifer, this is who I am—a cursed beast born to kill." Then he exited the vehicle.

Before he closed the door, he looked back once more. "Just so you know, I'm going to send you to your family the way I originally planned." He slammed the door, vanished for a moment, then reappeared at the front of the car with a gas can.

As gasoline splashed over the SUV, I frantically worked to free my hands. My muscles burned, but I pushed through, knowing my time was running out.

When the flames began to lick around the car, I finally broke free. Through coughs and pain, I managed to kick out the side window and worm my way out, landing hard on the icy pavement.

Rolling away from the blaze, I took a moment to recover, snow cooling my burns. I was battered, bruised, but alive—and determined to end this once and for all.

Chapter 3

October 13, 2014, 11:00 am EST

Charlotte, NC

Smoke filled my lungs in the darkness. I could hear screaming—my sister's scream. I opened my eyes, groggy and disoriented. Ahead of me, in the dark hallway, her bedroom door was partially open, her bedside lamp casting a dim glow. She was still making noise as I caught sight of a dark shape in her room.

My body and mind were addled, and the only thing driving me forward was the desire to help her. I had no idea how I'd ended up on the floor or what had happened leading up to this moment. All I knew was that I had to reach my sister. Just as I stretched out a hand to push the door open further, I heard breaking glass and saw something dark leap through it.

With the door now wide open, I could finally see the blood-soaked remains of my sister's body slumped on the floor, her head propped up by the nightstand. Her beautiful blue eyes were frozen in place, staring lifelessly like a doll's. I remember wanting to scream, but I couldn't; my coughing fits drowned out the sound, caused by the smoke billowing around me.

I looked back into the hallway. Fire had fully engulfed it. For some reason, I remember thinking how strangely beautiful it looked. I don't know what possessed me to climb out the window and fall two stories, but my mind and body were beyond rational thought at that point. At the hospital, the doctors told me I'd been bleeding out from a stab wound to the abdomen and had a mild concussion. Some of the nurses even said that angels must have lifted me out of that window.

I snapped out of my thoughts and realized I was sitting in my counselor's office, Dr. Crabtree, who was looking at me with a blank expression. I decided just to speak my mind.

***

"If there was a fair and just God watching over us, would He allow such evil?" I asked.

"Jenifer," Dr. Crabtree said, her green eyes probing mine gently. "It sounds like you're feeling an immense amount of pain, and it's completely natural to search for reasons or someone to hold accountable when faced with something so overwhelming. Sometimes, in the face of deep loss, it can feel like God or the universe has let us down. It can leave us feeling abandoned, questioning our beliefs, or wondering why something like this would happen. These feelings are more common than you might think and can be incredibly isolating."

Some of what she said made sense, I thought to myself, but at that moment, I was drawing a clear line in my mind. There was good, and there was evil, and I had just met one of the monsters.

"Is there anything else you'd like to share today,

Jenifer? Our time is almost up."

"No," I replied. All I wanted was to get out of that place, curl up in bed, and never wake up again. That's what I really wanted.

Ms. Crabtree spoke again as I stood up from the couch. "Jenifer, I know everything feels negative and bleak right now. I promise you, things will get better. It will just take time."

I don't remember exactly what I said, but I know I threw a string of curse words at her before storming out of her office, out of the clinic, and into my grandmother's waiting car at the curb.

At least Grandma understood that I didn't want to talk about my feelings. Oh, things would get better, alright. But how many years would it take? How long before I'd stop waking up from nightmares of my sister's dead eyes staring at me?

We must have driven around the city for about thirty minutes before Bobbie Jean Clayton, my grandmother, spoke up. "Are you getting hungry, dear?"

I just nodded. I honestly couldn't remember the last time I'd eaten. It wasn't that she hadn't cooked up something delicious, as she always did. I just couldn't bring myself to eat. But today, she parked right in front of Five Guys, knowing my weakness for a fresh burger and fries. How could I say no?

I devoured all of it, including some of her fries, and she even bought me a chocolate shake. In moments like these, I almost felt human again. Grandma just sat there, smiling as I ate. At the time, I didn't understand the pain she was going through. Just like me, she dealt with it by ensuring that I survived and moved forward.

There are so many things I wish I could have told her in those few years she pulled me out of the darkness. But I was so lost in my own grief, I couldn't see hers. I miss her so much and wish I could tell her how much I loved her just one more time.

The day after her funeral, I was old enough to get an apartment on my own. My old life was completely gone, but my hatred for the killer who had taken everything from me was still there. I began in earnest to find out who that son of a bitch was. The news had stopped reporting on him years ago, but that didn't mean he'd stopped.

People like the twenty-nine-day killer don't stop; they evolve. And so did I. A few years later, the killings began again in the States, and that's when I started my hunt. I swore to my sister—the one I see every night when I close my eyes—that I would bring justice for her and for our family.

Those cold, dead eyes blink at me once, and then she nods, silently acknowledging my promise. She never speaks before she disappears. But I know she's there, and then I fall asleep.

Chapter 4

October 28, 2024, 3:00 pm EST

I was aware that I had been in the hospital for several days now, with a police officer stationed just outside my room who avoided talking to me at all costs. The supermoon had happened the day before, and I remembered desperately trying to give the officer information I knew about the killer.

But I was restrained for my efforts. I'm not sure why I'm still alive. The effort of trying to rationalize it left me exhausted and frustrated, but nothing pissed me off more than not knowing what was happening. Surely, with what happened at the gas station, every cop in the state would be looking for this killer.

The TV in the room should have helped answer some of these questions, but it turns out the one in my room was busted, or so I was told. I immediately requested a room change but was rebuffed with the lame excuse that the other rooms were occupied.

My wounds made it difficult to get up and try to walk around. I had tried it several times. The doctor said I had been shot twice—once in the fatty part of my thigh, near my hip, and the other through my side and into my lung.

This was the one that had done the most damage and even now was hindering me from doing anything. I was forced to lie in that bed, replaying the events of that night at the station over and over in my mind. I was searching for clues and details I might have missed.

My mind hadn't been like this a few years ago. It had been a conscious choice on my part to learn how to look for the devil in the details. I remember reading every detective manual and magazine I could get my hands on. They taught me how to switch on my rational mind and apply deductive reasoning to what I observed.

I hadn't realized it at the time, but I had turned myself into a cold, calculating Sherlock Holmes. And there was comfort in living in that detached state. Emotions were suppressed so that clear thought could prevail. I was alive and had a purpose. All my friendships and support groups faded from my life. I didn't need them anymore. I had found my shield.

A knock at the door brought me out of my thoughts, and I turned to see the young deputy sheriff, Dan, entering my room with a small vase of flowers and a balloon that read "Get Well Soon."

I have to say, if it hadn't been for the gift, I would have probably ripped the man's head off.

"Good morning, miss," Dan said, placing the vase on a nearby nightstand.

"You mean afternoon?" I said. "And stop calling me 'miss.' My name is Jenifer."

He grinned, showing nice white teeth, and his pale blue eyes met mine. The deputy was attractive and charming in a subtle way. "You're right," he said. "How are you doing, Jenifer?"

"Shitty. No one has told me anything. Especially if the full moon slayer has been caught or not."

Dan's gaze instantly dropped to the floor, and I could see him rubbing his right hand against his pants leg. I could tell he was debating whether to tell me the truth or not, so I made the decision for him. "I would greatly appreciate the truth, Dan."

Those light blue eyes returned to mine as he moved closer. "The hunt for the serial killer is still on. The FBI was brought in, and just this morning a game warden found the site where the latest victims' bodies were left, or what was left of them." Dan's face went pale, and I thought he might actually throw up from what he was recalling.

"Have you been to the site?" I asked.

"No," he replied instantly. "I've seen photos."

"Any chance I could see them?"

He shook his head. "Like I said, there are a lot of people out looking for this killer. We will find him."

A painful chuckle erupted from my lips. "Do you know how many times I've heard those exact words? Or 'Oh, we're closing in and we have him in our sights.'"

"I'm sorry, Jenifer, I don't know what to say."

I wasn't really mad at him; I was just mad at the situation. More young girls' lives had been taken, and I had failed to stop him. "It's ok, Dan. I'm not mad at you. Would it be possible for my phone to be returned to me?"

He lowered his head and rubbed his cheek before speaking. "We couldn't find your phone at the scene. The FBI believes the killer took it, so they're monitoring it to see if it pops up on GPS."

"It's a good thing I kept no contacts on there," I said. And it was true. The only contacts were police officers and at least one FBI agent who halfway listened to me.

"I'm sorry about what happened at the gas station. I should have believed you. Then maybe the two of us could have taken this guy out."

"It's fine," I said. "If our roles had been reversed, I would have done the exact same thing. I don't blame you for that, Dan. And who knows? We both could have ended up dead instead of just injured and knocked unconscious."

He nodded but remained silent, just looking at me. It felt uncomfortable at first, but then I realized it felt good to get attention from such a good-looking man. I wondered if he was looking at me because he was attracted or if it was just pity because of my story.

"Maybe, once the doctor clears you, would you like to go out for coffee with me, Jenifer? There's a new specialty shop that opened just up the road, and the pumpkin spice is just right."

I stopped breathing for a second as my mind processed what had just happened. Had Dan just asked me out? What was going on? "Sure," I said, with a bit of hesitation. "That would be wonderful."

A smile broke across his face, and I could see those white teeth again. They weren't completely straight on the bottom, but his pale blue eyes and athletic build were just right. "Is there anything I can get for you, Jenifer? Books, magazines, or something to eat?"

For the first time in a long while, my mind felt foggy, and it was hard to concentrate. I should be taking advantage of this situation to see if I could get access to police information about the killer, but at this moment, none of that mattered.

"Thank you for the offer," I said. "I'm good for now. In fact, I'll probably lie back down and go to sleep after you leave."

Still smiling, he half-turned to walk away but stopped to say something. "I'll come back after I get off work this evening. I can bring your bag from the car."

"That would be wonderful, Dan. I look forward to seeing you again." As he turned to leave, I asked one last question. "Hey, Dan, in the gas station, where did the killer get your keys from?"

Dan turned around, rubbing the back of his head. "As soon as I entered the station, I heard a commotion going on in the laundry room near the arcade. I rushed to help but got hit in the back of the head and was knocked unconscious until the medics arrived."

"Any idea what was happening at the station? Why was everyone shooting at each other?" I asked.

"Turns out," Dan said, "someone found the poor waitress murdered in the kitchen. Then someone got shot, and that's when all hell broke loose."

"That's exactly what the killer wanted. He created chaos so he could steal one of the snowplows."

Dan nodded. "We found the plow miles up the road, abandoned near one of the forest reservations."

"Of course, he wasn't found?"

"No." Dan paused, looked at the door, then back at me. "The dead man in the car was a private investigator looking for the girl."

"I knew it," I exclaimed.

"Keep your voice down, Jenifer. What I'm telling you isn't public knowledge. I heard from the sheriff that the FBI determined the 29-day killer had an arrangement with the motel owner."

"So, it was one of his safe houses," I said.

"Looks like it. I also heard that the investigator was restrained and injected by the clerk personally. His fingerprints were found on the body and other things in the room. Sorry, but I have to run, Jenifer."

And then he left without another word. Feeling tired, I lay back down and closed my eyes, rationalizing what Dan had just told me. And I believed him, which made me excited about the prospect of having a date. Then, dark thoughts crept back in. *Do you know what kind of life you would be pulling this man into if the two of you became involved?* was the first question that plagued me.

Could you ever settle down, knowing the killer who took your family was still on the loose? You were so close to bringing him to justice. How can you let others continue to die and suffer?

These thoughts ran through my mind for hours until I fell asleep. I had no answers. On one hand, I wanted to stop the hunt and just be normal again. On the other, every time I closed my eyes, I saw the faces of every young girl this monster had killed since I started hunting him.

That's when the hunger returned. The need to avenge them. I had trained myself for years to hunt this monster. I couldn't quit now that I was so close. Granted, I had no idea where he would go next, now that the double full moon had passed.

His pattern would become random again as he bounced from state to state,

waiting for the next full moon in twenty-nine days. So, I had some time to figure things out.

Maybe I'd see how things played out with Deputy Dan.

Chapter 5

A day later, Dan was picking me up from the hospital and taking me to his aunt's house to stay until I recuperated enough to leave. The woman was in her mid-fifties and had a friendly manner.

In fact, she even offered hot tea and freshly baked chocolate chip cookies that tasted incredible. Of course, anything tasted better than the hospital food I had been forced to endure.

I would have spent more time with her, enjoying the casual conversation, but Dan had done something unexpected. He handed me a manila folder containing a copy of the most recent reports on the killings. The images were gruesome—what little I'd seen—and my mind was racing at the prospect of having firsthand information. There could be some clue here that would put me back on the trail.

I knew Dan could get in serious trouble for printing this for me, so I swore to him I would keep it a secret. I was so excited that I didn't know if I should kiss him or not. I decided to give him a peck on the cheek, then quickly hid the contents in my bag that he had brought.

Now, after excusing myself from his aunt, I was lying on a plush, comfortable bed with the folder open before me. Despite the gore of the high-definition pictures of the dead girls, excitement coursed through me. I was no longer laid up; I was back on the hunt. I was certain I could find the clues I needed to discern where the killer would strike next.

There were two dead girls in the photos, Kelly and Susan. They had been ripped open, their internal organs removed. It was known that the killer often chewed on the organs, like the heart and kidneys, sometimes consuming them entirely. The footprints at the scene were always distorted, likely due to something the killer wore to give the impression of beast-like, inhuman feet.

This pattern was consistent across the board. Everything the killer did was designed to create the illusion of being more than just a mentally ill man pretending to be a werewolf or skinwalker, as some had dubbed him.

I didn't believe either interpretation. This was just a very sick man; there was nothing supernatural about it. As to how he managed to keep getting away with it, there were a few factors at play. One, the man had to be wealthy, as he lived a transient lifestyle. One month he would kill a victim in North Carolina; the next, he would do it again in California.

This made him a hard target to catch. No one could ever pin him down to a specific state, much less a pattern. And attempts to narrow the search to protecting women at clubs and bars were futile, as some of his victims were students or businesswomen.

This led to the second part of my profile: the killer had to be an attractive enough man and act rationally enough to lure these women into his trap. There were some discrepancies, though. For instance, when I investigated the bar where Kelly had worked, her coworkers mentioned an older man who had been showing her a lot of attention before she went missing.

A similar situation happened with Brianna, a victim from several months ago in Florida. My theory was that the killer had a network of one or two people helping him, particularly with collecting victims and cleaning up crime scenes.

The scene in Florida had been badly contaminated before the police found it. Despite all the blood, not a single useful fingerprint was discovered, and no DNA matched any suspects.

The cops and FBI I told this theory to dismissed it, but I was convinced the killer didn't work alone. His wealth likely allowed him to keep those around him silent and compliant.

One report in the folder described how the kill site had been found by a local wildlife ranger. The location was deep in the woods, accessible only by a single fire road. Heavy rain had destroyed any tire or footprint impressions in the last few days.

I had been so absorbed in reviewing the files that I lost track of time and barely noticed the light knock on my bedroom door. "Jenifer," Dan's aunt said, "I made us some dinner if you're hungry."

At the mention of food, my stomach growled, and I realized the cookies from earlier were long gone. "I'll be down in a few minutes," I replied, shoving the papers back into the folder.

No new clues had jumped out at me yet, but there were still plenty of papers and photos to go through. Checking the clock on the nightstand, I saw it was 5:30 pm, meaning I had been working for at least four hours.

Hiding the folder in my pillowcase, I went downstairs to find Aunt Beth already sitting at the table, forking some salad from a bowl. The smell of spaghetti and garlic bread filled the air, and I was pretty sure my mouth watered at the thought of it.

I knew my stomach was excited because I felt it gurgling as I took my seat. Beth had set out three plates. From my brief observation of her and this place, I guessed she wasn't married anymore.

There were no photos of a man in the house, other than a few of Dan, and a faint discolored patch on her ring finger hinted at a recent divorce. Judging by the nicely framed diplomas near the entrance, I guessed she owned the house. I didn't have enough details to deduce her occupation, but I blamed that on the pain medication fogging my mind, along with the constant tiredness it caused.

"I hope you don't mind," Beth said. "Nothing I made has any meat in it."

"No, that's perfectly fine. Everything smells

wonderful. And thank you for agreeing to take care of me."

"It's no problem, my dear. I'm always glad to help my nephew out. It sounds like you two went through a terrible ordeal at that gas station. It's very fortunate both of you are still alive."

In truth, it was. I didn't answer her right away; instead, I focused on loading spaghetti onto my plate and grabbing a piece of garlic bread, which I shoved in my mouth. It was so good. I sat there, savoring the bread until it was gone.

Before diving into the spaghetti, I glanced at Beth, who had finished her salad and was sipping tea, observing me.

"This is so good," I said. "Thank you once again."

She gave me another smile. "Dan told me he thinks you both were attacked by the full moon slayer?"

I paused with noodles dangling from my fork, inches from my mouth. "Yes," I said.

Beth continued, "The paper that came out today—and even the news—has been reporting about that killer murdering a couple of young women nearby. I hope they catch his ass soon."

For reasons I couldn't explain, I chuckled slightly, earning a sharp look from her. "I'm not saying they won't catch him. It's just... they've been hunting him for years, and so far, I'm the only one who's gotten close enough to potentially kill him."

A silence fell between us until she spoke again. "Were you hunting this killer?"

I nodded. "I was his only surviving victim from ten years ago. He took everything from me—my sister, my family, my life."

Tears flowed down my cheeks, dripping off my chin. I didn't know why I had suddenly become so emotional. I had spent years in counseling and support groups, learning to suppress these feelings. For some reason, though, I let my guard down around this woman.

In my rational mind, I blamed this lapse on the medication. I would have to wean myself off it quickly, or I might end up curled up in a ball somewhere, overwhelmed by these emotions.

Aunt Beth didn't say anything back. Instead, she stood up, walked over to me, and wrapped me in the longest, warmest hug I could remember.

My body melded into it, and there was no stopping the tears now. The emotions were on full display, and I lacked the willpower to contain them.

At some point, between sobs, I heard the front door open and heavy footfalls approaching. Since Beth wasn't married, I reasoned it had to be Dan. I quickly pulled myself together, wiping my tears with a napkin.

Beth released me, and I looked up at those light blue

eyes.

"I didn't mean to interrupt," Dan said.

"It's all fine," Aunt Beth replied. "Please grab some food before you have to rush back to work."

"I am starving, but I wanted to check on you, Jenifer. How are you doing this evening?"

"Tired and hurting," I responded. It was the truth, though it didn't capture my anger and sadness. I shouldn't have let my emotions show like that. It was a huge mistake. "Please eat, Dan. Your aunt is an excellent cook."

"I know she is. That's why she leaves me a plate out when I work late." He sat down and loaded his plate with pasta and garlic bread.

Beth spoke up. "Any updates on catching the killer?"

Dan nodded. "The FBI is confident they're closing in."

I almost chuckled again at those words but restrained myself. That's FBI code for *we don't have a clue*, I thought.

"That's sad to hear. I've already counseled several new clients about this incident. The sooner that killer is caught, the better," Beth said.

"I couldn't agree more," Dan said between bites of garlic bread. "The whole town is in a frenzy over these killings. You have no idea how many bad leads I've had to follow because some neighbor thinks they know who the killer is."

Before I could stop myself, I blurted out, "The killer isn't from here, and he definitely wouldn't be staying here."

Dan gave me a pointed look. "I told my captain that, but we have to do our due diligence to the public."

"I get it," I said. "It makes them feel safer. In truth, in twenty-nine days, another young woman will be dead in some other town or city, and the local authorities will do the same thing there."

Silence descended at the table other than the scraping noises of Dan's fork on the plate. Once he was done, Aunt Beth grabbed up our plates and excused herself to the kitchen, before he spoke to me again.

"I know in your mind the authorities are not doing enough. I agree with you, Jenifer. Trust me, I wish I was doing more to hunt this killer. The truth is, once the FBI became involved, all our hands became tied."

Apologizing to Dan once again, I sat in silence as he got up and walked around the table toward me and then squatted down. With a lowered voice that only I could hear, he spoke. "Did you get a chance to look over the file I gave you?"

"Some of it. Thank you, by the way."

"You're welcome. Let me know if you come across anything you want me to investigate."

"Why, Dan? Are you offering to help me catch this killer?"

"What do you think?" he said with a smile. "I have some new evidence to show you." Producing his smart phone out of his jacket pocket, he showed me a dark video set in the woods.

My attention was fully drawn into it as I could see the outline of a woman falling to the ground in view of the camera. The details were blurry as a monstrous shadow of a thing leapt on top of her. Whatever it was didn't look human. It truly appeared to be some sort of large animal killing this woman. I was confused as to what I was looking at and then the video ended abruptly just after the thing finished gorging itself on internal organs.

"Was that supposed to be the killer?" I asked.

"It was the killer. A local bigfoot hunter had placed cameras on trees in that area. Before we knew it, he had posted this video all over the web. It's gone viral."

"That footage was so dark. I couldn't tell for sure what I was looking at."

"I assure you; it's legit. The FBI confirmed the timestamp and location of the camera that caught it. That was the killing of Kelly." He looked at the time on his phone and then stood back up. "Sorry, I got to go."

Nodding my head, I just sat there replaying that video in my mind over and over. What had I just seen? I knew the killer went to elaborate means to make people believe he was an honest to God werewolf. And this video would fool most into believing it.

Chapter 6

Over the next couple of days, I managed to get some rest, and with the help of painkillers, I was beginning to feel like myself again. Dan's aunt didn't turn out to be the person I thought she might be. After my breakdown with her, I had half-expected her to force me out of the house after a day or two.

Instead, she continued to be friendly and attentive, even taking me shopping for a new phone and buying me some new clothes along the way. I wouldn't call our relationship a friendship exactly; it almost felt more like a grandmotherly love. Whatever it was, I felt comfortable and at peace, which was something I hadn't felt in a very long time.

As for Dan, he kept me updated on any new developments in the case, but as I knew, the killer was long gone from here, and the countdown to the next full moon was underway.

Most of the locals were still terrified by the recent events, and the mayor had enacted a county-wide curfew.

The video that a local had captured of the killing had not only made him famous, but major news stations had picked it up, and suddenly the twenty-nine-day killer was more notorious than ever.

It was disgusting, in my opinion. This murderer had suddenly been elevated to the status of a famous serial killer. I was sure someone was already planning to make a movie about it. I tried not to think about it, and Dan did his best to provide distractions.

In fact, his aunt decided to go visit a friend for the evening, giving Dan and me a chance to have some private time. Dan arrived shortly after 5 p.m., and the sun was already setting for the evening. We had agreed on Chinese food—mostly Lo Mein and two bottles of soda.

The taste of Mountain Dew was so sweet and sugary in my mouth that I just wanted to keep sipping it for the rest of the night. Aunt Beth didn't believe in sodas and only kept bottled water, tea, and a single bottle of wine in the refrigerator, which was often replaced.

I didn't judge her for it; she was the nicest person I'd dealt with in years, and I was enjoying my stay.

"I didn't know what kind of movie to get at Redbox, so I got two different comedies," Dan said as he stood in front of the TV in the living room. "I figured horror movies would be a bad idea."

I nodded in agreement as I tore into the Lo Mein. I wasn't sure if it was because I felt comfortable here, but I was honestly eating more than I think I ever had in my life.

The rational side of me was screaming to regain control and not eat so much, but it was also telling me I should have left these people and this place a long time ago.

I justified my decisions by reminding myself that the killer was long gone from this area, and with several days left until the next full moon, he was probably stalking his newest prey even now.

Dan plopped down beside me on the couch and scooped his own Lo Mein into a bowl, attempting to use chopsticks. I couldn't tell if he was trying to impress me or just make me laugh, but watching him struggle with them was like watching a baby eat as it smeared food everywhere.

"There are some forks in the bag," I said, holding back a laugh.

He slowly lowered the bowl to his lap. "Yeah, I should probably use a fork. I thought I'd mastered the chopsticks this time."

"You just need a little more practice," I said, grinning.

He had such a serious look on his face as he took the fork in hand. I couldn't tell if he was genuinely trying to master chopsticks or just being playful—until he flashed a grin before diving back into the Lo Mein.

Within a few minutes, we had devoured the entire container and set our bowls aside. We sat back, watching whatever movie this was. Honestly, I had no clue, and I was pretty sure Dan didn't either, because what started as holding hands soon turned into us snuggling on the couch, kissing.

The feel of his hand running down my back sent shivers up my spine. Our lips pressed together, our tongues gently caressing and exploring, sending my body into a euphoric excitement I had never felt before.

All thoughts of restraint or control had flown out the window. I could feel myself melting into his body, and I was losing myself to his desire. God, why did it feel so good?

His hand slipped under my shirt, inching toward one of my breasts. I wanted him to touch me, to squeeze me, to lose himself with me.

Things were escalating rapidly out of my control, and I was okay with it because I wanted him. I wanted everything.

A loud banging on the door snapped us both out of the moment, and Dan looked up, seeing the flashing blue lights through the windows. "Dan," a voice shouted from the other side of the door. "We need to talk; there's been another killing."

We both got up from the couch and straightened ourselves before Dan opened the door. On the other side was another young deputy, his cheeks red, his face somber. "Dan, I've been trying to reach you."

"What's happened, Ryan? Who's been killed?"

The other deputy paused, sucking in a breath. "Your

Aunt Beth and Ethel Chadwick are dead."

I felt myself collapse to my knees. It wasn't possible; the killer never stayed in the same area. Had I brought this down upon his aunt? Was she dead because of me?

Dan was nearby, reaching out a hand toward me. He was speaking, but it took a moment for me to focus enough to understand his words. "Jenifer, this is not your fault. We don't even know if it was the killer."

For some reason, I took his hand and let him help me back to my feet. He was right; this couldn't have been the killer. And I could help him figure out who had done this.

Chapter 7

The ride to the Chadwick house wasn't long. In fact, it was just right up the road in an old two story Victorian house. That had been refurbished and well cared for. Dan was riding in the back of the police SUV with me. We were holding hands tightly and I could see from his constant looking around that his mind was looking for anything to focus on.

I couldn't blame him. I was sad, I was hurting from the news. However, I had learned to divorce myself from these feelings a long time ago. The only thing still gnawing at me was the fact that this had all been my fault. As soon as I had gotten out of the hospital, I should have hit the road.

Instead, I allowed myself to falsely believe that my fate had changed. That I had a chance at a normal life. Instead, the killer had singled me out. He had failed to kill me twice now. And that either put him into a rage or perhaps something else.

After reviewing the evidence in my mind, the second attempt on my life had not been fatal, because the killer hadn't wanted it to be. He spared my life for some reason.

So was the killing of the aunt the purpose for sparing me. He wanted to continue stalking and harassing me now.

It was cold to view it this way, but if this is what the killer's mindset had become, then he was setting himself up to be caught. I could turn this to my advantage, but first, I needed to distance myself from Dan. I could no longer jeopardize him for this quest. I would finish it on my own, just as I had started. And this time, I would finish the job.

Dan squeezed my hand hard before letting go. He was opening his door and stepping toward the Chadwick house. I could see cops and deputies all over the place. Some were providing crowd control as a few neighbors had ventured out of their houses to find out what was going on.

Others were taking photographs and writing down notes. It was unusual for me to be on a crime site the same day it happened. Ever since taking on the responsibility of taking down this killer, I often had to visit these sites late at night and as stealthily as possible in order to figure out any possible clues for myself.

The cops, with rare exception, would share nothing with me. Much less answer any questions. Dan had been the first to be so open with me about the investigation. I will save him any further trouble of pain and suffering by slipping out of the house late tonight.

I don't know where I will go, but far away was good. That would force the killer to follow me. Dan stood stone still on the porch, looking in the house, when I caught up beside him. The rain had turned from a light drizzle to a significant downpour now. And I heard it pounding heavily on the roofing. He looked back at me once, nodded his head, and stepped into the house.

I followed right behind him. Right at the entrance was the stairway to the upper floor. The most activity was coming from the room to the left-hand side. I followed Dan through the hallway covered in photographs of a loving family with several kids.

The photos gave a sort of timeline. The first ones closest to the door were of young kids, but as I proceeded, the ages of the kids and family increased. When I reached the last one it was my guess that both the son and daughter were of the age to be in college now. So that explained why they were not home.

The husband in every photo, even vacation ones, was always dressed in button ups and a tie. He was obviously a professional man of some sort. And made the money since this house would not have been cheap and from the UNC monogram on the son's shirt, they could afford to send them to good colleges.

I was in the zone, taking in every detail I came across. I was more determined than ever to bring this killer to justice. All my deductive reasoning came to a sudden halt once I reached the living room. What had made me lose my concentration wasn't the sight of two covered bodies on the floor.

It had been the message written on the white wall where the TV had once been. For some reason, the killer had addressed it to me. *Jenifer Leigh Walker*, the message had begun in blood. At first, I had thought the killer had used his finger to write with. But the closer I got to it, I realized that the killer had used a brush dipped in blood.

When we crossed paths the other night, at first I saw you as a threat to my life. Now I realize that we are kindred spirits. Fated to belong to one another. I know you felt it too. So let's stop pretending about who we really are.

Signed *JBT* down at the bottom. There was something significant about this signature. The J and the T had special loops in them with a slight curve at the tails. I had seen this signature before, but where?

Lost in thought, rummaging through my mind as to where I might have seen this signature, I was startled by a hand touching me on the shoulder. I jumped in surprise and was about to slam my elbow into whoever's face was behind me. Fortunate for Dan, he was talking to me at the same time as he was touching, which negated the beating I was about to deliver to him.

"Are you ok?" He asked.

"No," I said with a shake of my head. My eyes kept drawing back to the note and the initials.

"This is not your fault," he said, with his hand still on my shoulder. I could feel him squeezing it gently. Despite my detached state, I could feel anger welling up inside of me. I tried to take a deep breath, but words just erupted out of my mouth.

"Of course it's my fault," I said. "Just look at the damn note. The killer thinks we are soul mates." I didn't give Dan any time to respond back to me. I had to get out of the house. I had to find my calm and center. And I walked out into the rain and just kept walking.

October rain in North Carolina is never warm, and I

had no idea how long I had been walking before Dan pulled up beside me in the SUV. "Jenifer, please get into the vehicle. Let me get you warm."

I was already warm on the inside. My rage was like a volcano, right on the edge of erupting. Outwardly, my arms were crossed and held tight to my chest, and my teeth were chattering. Walking helped me to regain focus, but in this instance, I agreed that I needed to warm up before I found myself back in the hospital again.

Dan remained silent until we got back to his aunt's house. He helped me inside and ordered me to stripe by the door as he went and got some towels. At first, I thought about refusing, but then realized the logic in the ask.

The floor beneath me had turned into a puddle that was creeping into the thick white carpet. If I had gone upstairs like this, I would have left a wet mess all the way to my room. And I certainly didn't want to do that. It would have been disrespectful.

When Dan came back with a couple of large towels in hand. I snatched one up and began to dry off my naked body. I could feel him watching me. Despite the trauma of the day, there was a hunger there. I could see it in his eyes when I glanced up at him. He was focused on my breasts.

For reasons I cannot explain to myself, I found myself stepping toward him. Wanting to be in his warm embrace again. And he wrapped me up with our lips meeting again. After a long and passionate kiss we found ourselves back on the couch as before, but this time, Dan had removed his shirt between each kiss and the rest was a magical escape from the sorrows of the day.

I don't think I had ever slept so deeply than I did in

his embrace. Because when I awoke the next morning, the sun was high in the sky. There were people out and about walking dogs or pushing babies in strollers. I couldn't see them so much as I could hear them. Dan was still asleep, but I awoke him as I tried to crawl out of his embrace. His eyes went wide when he looked down at his phone.

"I got to get ready," he said. "I have a shift this afternoon."

"I'm sure they will understand if you take the day off," I said, watching him scramble about trying to straighten out his clothes from the night before.

"I need to run by my house and change. I wish I had time to have breakfast with you, but I'm going to be late as is."

"Dan, it's ok. Take a deep breath and just relax."

Look at me, giving advice on how to calm oneself down. Didn't work yesterday, I thought to myself.

After throwing on his shirt and pants, he gave me a kiss on the lips and then paused long enough at the door to say something. "I'll swing by during my break and bring us something to eat. Love you." And then he was gone out the door.

Dan's words lingered in the air long after he left: "Love you." It wasn't the words themselves that shattered me—it was the warmth behind them. The promise of safety and a life I'd longed for but never believed I could have. I wanted to love him back, to hold onto this fleeting sense of normalcy. But love meant danger now, and every moment I stayed, I increased his chances of becoming the next target.

I sat on the edge of the couch, running my fingers over the soft fabric where we'd shared moments of comfort, then stood up abruptly. I couldn't afford to let emotions cloud my judgment, not now. My hands trembled as I packed my few belongings, but I forced myself to keep moving. I scribbled a quick note on a piece of paper: "I'm sorry, Dan. I have to finish this alone."

An hour later, I had what few things that belonged to me in a grocery bag standing by the main door, looking back at the living room and kitchen. It felt important to have one last look to cement the good memories I had here. Then I walked out the door to a waiting Uber that would take me to my car at the gas station, where I had left it parked.

Along the way, I closed my eyes and allowed my mind to drift back in time. I was looking for whatever had triggered my memory about the initials the killer had left. At first there was nothing but frustration, but when I remembered signing in at the mental clinic I was sent to after the incident with my family.

Those initials on the sign in clipboard lit up like a neon sign. It was an exact match. The killer had been local and had even been seeing a psychiatrist at the same place I was.

I now knew where to go and I would at last know who this killer was.

Chapter 8

Yellow police tape still marked the back half of the gas station, and the damaged sections were now boarded up to keep out the unpredictable weather. Truckers were pulling in to fuel up, and I needed gas myself, but I decided to get further down the road.

The drive to Charlotte was only a couple of hours down I-77, but I was cutting it close to hitting five o'clock traffic, which could easily add another hour or two to my trip. I wasn't even sure why I still kept an apartment there. I hadn't spent much time in the city over the past year.

I followed the path of the killer, and, as luck would have it, the money I was awarded by the insurance companies was more than enough to continue my pursuit. I figured I would settle into a normal job once justice had been served. Frankly, I didn't even know what I wanted to do.

The time and effort I'd spent developing my skills would be wasted in retail or at a grocery store. I had considered a career as a detective or an investigator for prosecutors. I was sure they could use someone with my talents.

Who knew how long I'd be waiting to pursue any of

those professions. Right now, I needed to buckle down and figure out a way to get the information I needed. The clinic wasn't too far from the apartment, but they certainly wouldn't allow me to go through their patient records.

I could try to bribe one of the clerks—money had a way of making people do things they shouldn't. But if I or the clerk got caught, we'd both be facing prison time, and I didn't have time for that.

The only other approach I could think of was to talk to the counselor who had helped me. Maybe if I told her what had happened and what I'd discovered, she might be willing to look into it. I looked her up on my phone and found out that Miss Crabtree had moved to a different state and was working for a high-end company now.

So that avenue was closed. Breaking and entering was off the table, so I had one card left to play. There was a police detective named Woodrow who kept up with me from time to time, so I gave him a call.

To my surprise, the man picked up on the third ring. "Detective Woodrow," he said.

"Hi, Detective," I replied, a little hesitantly. "This is Jenifer Walker."

There was a brief silence on the other end, and I was half tempted to check my phone to see if he'd hung up, but then he spoke again. "Good to hear from you, Jenifer. Is everything okay?"

"Not exactly. You know about that incident at the gas station about three weeks ago?"

"Don't tell me you were involved in that, Jenifer. There were about half a dozen bodies recovered there."

I didn't know the exact count of the dead; it hadn't seemed relevant at the time. Now that Woodrow had put it into perspective, that body count was staggering. "He was there, Detective. I almost had him."

"Jenifer," Woodrow began, his tone dropping to something almost fatherly. "I know you want to catch this killer, but you're throwing your life away by chasing him. You need to let go before he claims you as a victim again."

"It's too late for that. He almost succeeded in killing me this time. Except he decided to leave me alive. Now he's taunting me, showing his intentions by killing someone I knew outside of his usual cycle."

"I don't understand," Woodrow said. "Who else did he kill, and where?"

"I'll explain everything, Detective, but I need you to trust me when I say that I now know who the killer is."

"So, who is it?" he asked, his voice tense.

"At the last crime scene, not even a day ago, he wrote a note in blood on a wall, addressed to me, with his initials. There was something familiar about them, and my mind went into overdrive trying to remember where I'd seen those unique initials before. I have a picture of it on my phone—I'll send it to you."

"That would be perfect. So, where had you seen them?"

"After the incident with my family, I started seeing a

counselor at a nearby clinic. I remember seeing those exact initials on one of the sign-in sheets."

Woodrow paused, then spoke. "I'm looking at the picture you sent. And you're right—those initials are unique. I take it you want me to look into this?"

"I was hoping you could get a court order so we could find out who this person is from the clinic."

"I can try, Jenifer, but honestly, I'll need more proof before a judge lets me dig into confidential files. It could take time."

I knew this would be a waste of time. In my experience with law enforcement, everything slowed down to a snail's pace because of bureaucracy. What the detective was really saying was that it could be months before he'd get approval to search those files. "I don't have that kind of time, Detective."

"Wait, listen to me, Jenifer. The evidence you found and its connection are groundbreaking, but I need you to trust me and follow the process. We *will* catch this killer."

"You realize that in two days he'll kill again?" I raised my voice, needing him to understand the urgency. Another young woman was going to lose her life, and then he'd go back to taunting me. There was no telling who he'd kill to get close to me again.

"I understand. The FBI has taken over the case, and I'll bring them this evidence as well. All you need to do, Jenifer, is to find a safe place to lay low while we do our jobs."

I wasn't sure which words set me off, but I found myself punching the end call button. I couldn't sit this one out. I was so close to knowing who the killer was. A plan began to form in my mind.

Two hours later, I pulled into the parking lot of the clinic. I knew this was where I'd find the information I needed. There were no cameras outside, just inside, which were the ones I had to worry about. After mentally reviewing several plans, I realized there was no way I could pull this off without giving away my identity.

So, I got out of my car, checked the taser and lighter in my pockets, and headed inside. The place hadn't changed at all in the last few years. The waiting area was still lined with seats along the white walls, now decorated with a few pictures here and there.

Someone had finally added plants, which helped break up the stark white from the fluorescent lights, tile floors, and walls. When I first came here, I often wore my shades inside. Today was no different as I approached the glass protecting the sign-in station along the far wall. To the left was a door leading into the office hallway, and to the right, another door led to the sign-in room and the nearby records room.

I knew this layout because my counselor had given me a grand tour one day, probably to help make the place feel less institutional.

"Miss," an older Black woman at the window called out to me. "I need you to sign in."

I hadn't seen this woman before; she was a new

addition. I picked up the pen and scribbled my name. She took it without another word, but I knew it wouldn't take her long to realize I wasn't on anyone's schedule for the day.

I headed toward the women's bathroom on the far left-hand side of the sign-in window. First, I checked the stalls to make sure they were empty, then I peeked back outside to see if anyone was approaching.

With the coast clear, I took the lighter out and set some paper in the trash bin on fire, then casually walked back out and sat as far from the bathroom as possible. Within moments, the woman at the sign-in station started calling my name, just before someone screamed, "Fire!"

The fire alarm was pulled, and people rushed toward the entrance. I watched until I saw the woman from the sign-in station leave through a side door with others. I don't think anyone noticed me moving toward the door to the office.

I had the taser gripped firmly in hand, and I walked up behind the woman, shocking her in the back. She jerked from the shock, then collapsed into my arms. Quickly, I stashed the taser and searched her for keys to the records room. I'd taken a gamble that she'd have keys, and fortunately, I was right. Someone took her from me to help her outside, and I slipped through the now-empty door.

The keys worked perfectly—until I reached the records door, where they didn't fit. I wasn't going to be stopped now. I grabbed a small fire extinguisher from the wall and slammed it against the door handle until it snapped off.

Once the guts of the lock were exposed, it was no

problem to open the door. I could hear sirens in the distance, and I knew my time was short. I quickly located the filing cabinet marked with the killer's last initial and dove into it.

Whoever maintained these files was meticulous. Everything was alphabetical, making it easy to find the name: Justin Bartholomew Tompkins. I double-checked to ensure there were no other names with matching initials. As the sound of firefighters drew closer, I knew it was time to go.

I tucked the folder under my shirt, securing it in my pants to keep it in place, and headed for the exit. A firefighter spotted me but just told me to clear the area quickly.

I complied, walking right out the front door, past a crowd of onlookers, and made it back to my car without a hitch. Now was no time to celebrate. I drove off and found a fast-food parking lot a few miles away, where I began digging through the file.

In bold print, in the doctor's own words: "Justin is a very disturbed young man who continues to resist our medications and even shock therapy, which helped at first but then made his delusions worse. He believes he is some sort of creature—perhaps a werewolf."

"Son of a bitch," I muttered. "The bastard knew." How could this doctor not put two and two together about the killings and the full moon connection? As I kept going through the file, I found my answer.

Shortly after the third victim of the 29-day killer, all the doctor's notes abruptly stopped, and someone had inserted an obituary from the paper. The doctor's life had ended the night after the third victim, Shelly, had been killed.

I remembered it well because right after Shelly, the 29-day killer disappeared for a couple of years. Many thought his reign of terror was over, but I knew better. There were similar killings in Mexico before he returned to the States.

The folder provided every detail I needed: where the killer grew up, and where his wealthy parents lived. They resided in a gated community in the SouthPark district of Charlotte, reserved for high-income families. That was where I had to go next—and quickly, before anyone figured out what had happened at the clinic.

I estimated I had at least a few hours before the police were on to me. Hopefully, it would be enough time to find out where the killer was. I was certain his parents knew; after all, it was likely their money protecting him. Now, I just needed a way to get into that gated community and confront them.

Seeing a Domino's pizza delivery vehicle pass by on the main road, an idea struck me.

Chapter 9

I followed the pizza driver all the way back to his store just up the road. I was still many miles from the Tompkins house, but I had a plan and a powerful motivator to get what I wanted. I parked near the delivery cars, gathered the essentials I needed into my handbag, and waited for one of the drivers to come out.

The first one was a young woman, and I decided against approaching her. But the second was a young man with long hair and acne. I guessed his age to be around seventeen or eighteen, give or take a year or two. Guessing someone's age had never been my strong suit, but I had spent countless hours watching crime TV and paying close attention to body language and facial expressions.

It's amazing how quickly one can learn to observe behaviors. I felt I'd developed a pretty good proficiency at spotting lies, something I'd put to the test more often than one might think.

I got out of my car and approached the young man, who didn't even notice me until I was almost right on top of him.

"You scared the hell out of me," he said, nearly dropping the pizzas onto the pavement.

"Sorry," I said, trying to sound embarrassed. "I was hoping to ask a favor. I know you don't know me, but I could really use your help."

His cheeks turned red as he responded. "I'm kind of busy with deliveries, but I'm willing to hear you out."

"Have you ever delivered to the Stonecrest gated community before?" I asked.

"No," he replied quickly.

"How about any gated community?"

He nodded. "Sure, there's a couple over by the lake. They let me in. What's this all about?"

I moved in closer to him. I wasn't someone who usually used my femininity on a young man to get what I wanted. Well, at least not normally. Dan had been the first real man I'd been with. Everyone else from before had been just boyfriends who quickly disappeared after the incident. I couldn't blame them.

"I was hoping you could do me a favor, and I'll make it worth your time." I pulled out five hundred dollars from my bag.

He glanced at the cash, but his eyes lingered on my chest, so I moved even closer, which almost made him drop the pizzas again.

"Sure," he said, taking the cash from my hand. "Hop in."

The car was a fairly new Honda. He had a pine tree air

freshener hanging from the mirror, but the smell of pizza was overpowering. I had to admit, I probably would have scarfed down a slice if offered.

"So, what's the story?" he asked, glancing over at me.

I gave him the hard-luck story I'd come up with in my car. "I have assholes for parents. Just because I got busted for underage drinking and a few other things, they kicked me out. I need to get back inside so I can grab some clothes—and especially the money I've been hiding for this kind of situation."

"I'm sorry to hear that," he said. "My name's Ted, and I understand about hard-nosed parents. Whatever you need, I'm willing to help out."

Is it possible to feel sick at one's own actions but excited at the same time? I was definitely past the threshold of staying within the law, and I saw no point in trying to redeem myself yet—not until I'd brought Justin to justice, whatever that might look like.

"Do you have an extra hat?" I asked. That would at least help me look like a pizza worker.

Ted reached into the back seat while still driving and pulled out a blue Domino's hat. It had sweat stains on the inside and a sour smell. I put it on anyway; I was already committed to this path.

A few minutes later, we arrived at the guard booth for the community. I had already given Ted the address and name of the family.

"Who are you delivering to?" the middle-aged guard asked, peering into the car and looking around.

"The Tompkins at 612 Ash Street," Ted said.

"It's unusual for them to order pizza at this time of day," the guard said, locking his gaze on me. His eyes were cold and dark, making me fidget. "Why do you have another person with you?"

Ted didn't waste any time responding. "New manager in training. The big boss wants her to see the routes and locations we deliver to."

The guard's gaze shifted from mine, which I was grateful for. There was a moment of hesitation before he spoke. "Open the big pizza bag."

By this point, there were at least two cars behind us, and one of them was getting impatient, honking the horn. "I said, open the pizza bag."

Ted reached back into the back seat and brought the red insulated bag to the front, placing it in my lap. I knew that if the guard checked the addresses on the pizza boxes, we'd both be busted, but what could I do?

Just as Ted was about to open the flap, exposing the addresses, the guard backed off as a voice boomed over his radio. "Marshall, what the hell is going on down there? I've got two lawyers blowing up my phone saying they can't get home because you're holding up a pizza delivery."

"Sir, I'm just doing my job, making sure our clients are safe."

"Sargeant, this isn't a military post. Let's get these people home before they sue all of us."

"Understood, sir," the guard said, waving us through

the gate.

"Well, that was intense," Ted said. "Most gate guards don't even bother checking the addresses."

I breathed a sigh of relief as Ted pulled up in front of a beautiful three-story house with a grand stone stairway leading down to the left side.

"I have one last request," I said.

Ted looked over at me.

"I'm going to take one of the pizza boxes and go to the door. I need you to drive around the block for a couple of minutes before coming back here." I thought he'd question me, but he simply said, "Okay."

I got out of the car with a pizza in one hand and my taser hidden under the box in the other. I watched Ted drive off, then rang the doorbell. My heart was pounding, my body shivering slightly. I took several deep breaths to keep my nerves under control.

An older woman in business attire opened the door. Without giving her a chance to speak, I thrust the pizza box at her face, which opened her torso to my taser. I had no idea who she was, but I'd find out soon enough. I just needed to get inside.

The woman collapsed backward onto the ornate tile floor, the pizza box skidding open but keeping its contents inside. I closed the door behind me and stood still for a moment, listening.

Once I was certain there was no one else in the house,

I left the woman and began searching around. I knew I'd have a few minutes before she could move again, so I used that time to gather information.

The living room was immediately to the right, as grand as the rest of the house. I didn't care about the decor; I was more interested in the few sparse pictures. The main photograph on the wall was an older picture of the woman I'd tased, along with a well-dressed husband, a young daughter, and a young boy.

In more recent photos, the daughter had disappeared, and only the boy was shown at various ages. I checked my phone for the time and headed upstairs.

The first room I entered was a young girl's room. Everything was clean and in place, almost like a shrine. It seemed the family hadn't let go of the daughter's memory.

The next room was dark, covered in band posters with large speakers in each corner. Typical young man's room, I thought. But on closer inspection, I noticed unusual scratch marks on the floor and on the wooden bedposts. There had even been hasty attempts to buff them out, but the marks were still obvious.

Several places in the room had been patched over, except for one spot on the floor, where there was evidence of an anchor point, as if a chain had been run through it. This explained some of the scratch marks.

Had they tried to restrain the boy on full moons? Were they playing into his delusion? I would have my answer soon as I rushed back downstairs.

When I returned, the woman was lying on the floor, gasping for breath and convulsing. This was bad—there was nothing I could do for her except call for an ambulance. I'd already done terrible things, but I didn't want to add murder to the list.

I dialed 911 and walked out the front door, hoping Ted had already come back around. Thankfully, he had, and I rushed to the car.

"Get me out of here," I said urgently.

"What happened?" Ted asked.

"I don't want to talk about it," I replied, my heart pounding and my hands shaking. I tried to take deep breaths, focusing on calming down until we cleared the gatehouse. Once we were back on the main roads, I closed my eyes.

Ted was nice enough not to ask more questions until we got back to the pizza place. "I know we just met," he said. "If you ever need help again or just someone to talk to, I'll be there."

Before getting out of the car, I gave him a quick peck on the cheek, then slowly walked back toward my car, head down, replaying the details of the day in my mind. I knew I'd broken many laws and would likely serve time for it.

I'd justified all my actions on the

chance of learning where Justin was. If I could just bring him to justice, everything would be worth it. I knew Dan wouldn't approve, but I hoped he'd forgive me someday.

I really did care for him. By the time I reached my car door, I barely noticed the black SUV that pulled up behind me. Suddenly, someone grabbed me from behind, pressing a cloth over my mouth.

Whoever it was had the element of surprise. Desperately, I struggled to break free, but I felt myself losing consciousness.

Chapter 10

Everything was a blur when I first opened my eyes. After several blinks, things began to come into focus, and my awareness of my situation fully hit me. My arms were restrained above my head by a chain, and my ankles were cuffed together. I was trussed up like a pig to be slaughtered.

To my surprise, I wasn't gagged. Had this been an oversight on my captors' part, or were they just that confident in the isolation of this place? Everything was dark and damp. I had a sense that I was underground somewhere, but the lighting was so poor I couldn't make out any details around me.

Then a voice boomed from behind. I tried turning my head to see who was talking, but the voice stayed out of sight. "You've been a very bad girl, Jenifer. Breaking into places and even nearly killing Miss Thompkins. To be honest, we would have probably let you get away with the other stuff, but not with an attack on our benefactor."

Silence followed. I realized there were at least two people with me, confirmed by two different sounds: someone drawing a blade and someone cracking their knuckles.

"Sorry, Jenifer, but we can't let you keep roaming around causing more trouble for the family."

The words that followed weren't intentional; they came from a place of rage that had been building within me. "You're the little pieces of shit who follow him around, cleaning up his messes and bringing him new victims every twenty-nine days?"

This time, instead of a disembodied voice, an older man with graying hair and steely gray eyes got right up in my face, pressing a long knife against my throat. "For someone so pretty, it's amazing how clever you are. The cops still seem clueless about everything."

"They won't be now," I said, raising my voice. "Not after they start putting the evidence together from today."

The man backed away, laughing, and another voice, still out of sight, joined in.

"And tell me, Jenifer. What do you think you accomplished today? Never mind, I'll tell you. First off, the cops will investigate the clinic and the Tompkins' house, and all they'll find is a family with a slightly disturbed son who witnessed his sister's brutal killing by a pack of wolves during a camping trip with Mr. Tompkins in Romania."

That explained the sudden disappearance of the daughter from the photographs and also shed light on Justin's obsession with wolf-like behaviors and perhaps the werewolf myths. "You're wrong," I said. "Smart cops will start to piece things together, and they'll bring you down and make you pay for all the murders."

The man walked right back up to me, placing the knife back at my throat. "If Justin had had us around from the start, then he wouldn't have a little pest like you dancing around causing problems. I would've made sure you were dead and burned in that house."

Before I knew what I was doing, I spat right into the man's face. He wiped it away slowly, a smile spreading across his face.

"You know, I had thought about killing you quickly, with very little pain, but I think I've changed my mind. We're going to have a little fun, you and me."

"How about you take these restraints off, and we'll see how much of a real man you are."

"Damn, you're just making this too much fun."

"Before you start, tell me how he fakes his crime scenes. Does he wear prosthetics to emulate the footprints? Or do you guys follow up and create the scene?"

The man leaned in so close that our noses were touching. "You really don't know, do you? It's no act."

"Bullshit," I said. "There's no such thing as werewolves or shapeshifters or skinwalkers." I watched as he backed up, using the knife to scratch at his stubbly beard.

"I guess you'll never know for certain," he said, and then he began to cut my shirt open.

My mind raced desperately, searching for anything I could say or do to delay my death, but rational thought left me. I was in full-blown panic mode, my heart racing, my body trembling. All I could do was place my mind somewhere else—a place of fond memories, where my family was, and where I was happiest. The smell of the ocean and a cool summer breeze blowing across my skin. I was standing on the beach, my bare feet digging into the sand. My younger brother was trying to build a sandcastle too close to the water. My parents were walking hand in hand along the shoreline, and my older sister was out in the water, trying to catch a wave with a bodyboard.

She loved the ocean. My father had even booked her surfing lessons that week. I could stand there all day, and nothing could hurt me. No pain, no suffering.

A loud noise shattered my peaceful vision, jolting me back to reality. The noise happened again, and I saw the older man on the ground, bleeding and scooting away, one hand raised in surrender.

"We had to do something about her," the man was pleading. "She was going to expose all of us."

A figure appeared to my left. I could only make out a black outline, but it looked like they held a shotgun. "I told you, she was off-limits."

"We were trying to protect you. You need us."

"I don't need anyone," the man with the shotgun shouted. The voice sounded deeper, but I was certain it was Justin. He walked up to the older man, placed the shotgun barrel against his chest, and pulled the trigger.

I closed my eyes instinctively, not wanting to see the blood and gore. But I was forced to open them again when I felt someone's heavy breath close to my face. Those jade-green eyes met mine.

"I'm sorry, Jenifer," Justin said softly. "They were told not to harm you."

A flood of questions rushed through my mind, but I kept silent, hoping Justin's delusional state might lead him to set me free.

"It's okay, Justin. Thank you," I said, hoping my words would calm him, but instead, he stopped moving and stared at me intently.

"So, you know my name now. Did one of them tell you?"

"No," I said, forcing a smile. "You left your initials for me on that note you wrote on the wall. Did you really think I wouldn't figure it out?"

A smile broke across his face. He was young, with long, dark, unkempt hair and a few days' worth of stubble on his chin. "No, I knew you'd figure it out. I wanted you to."

"It was fortunate you showed up in time to save me from these men. How did you know I was in trouble?"

"I've been tracking you since you got your new

phone."

Wait—how was that possible? I'd changed my number, and there shouldn't have been a way for him to track me. "How?"

He took a step closer, still smiling. "I went to the stores that serviced your carrier. Using info I got from your old phone, I convinced several clerks that you were my wife and that I thought you were cheating on me. I paid them a little up-front fee, and they agreed to send me your new number and the ID needed to track it."

A string of curse words sat on the tip of my tongue, ready to unleash, but I bit them back, taking a deep breath. I couldn't let my emotions get the better of me now. My best chance was to keep playing along and wait for the right moment to escape.

"It's amazing what a few hundred-dollar bills can do for you."

How true that was. I'd used similar tactics recently. Was I becoming like this monster? Had I crossed too many lines?

"I know you still have many questions for me, and I swear I'll answer them. But not until you've seen the true me—the thing that drives my soul. Tomorrow night, you will meet him, and he will judge your worth."

At some point, he'd produced a syringe, and before I could react, he injected me with it. As my consciousness began to slip, my last thoughts were of Dan and me holding hands on his aunt's couch. It had been the happiest moment in my life recently, and I wished for nothing more than to go back to that moment and stay there forever.

Chapter 11

I woke up in the darkness, cold and disoriented. My vision was blurred, but I could make out the sound of two women talking nearby. I tried to speak, but all that came out was a hoarse croak.

My throat felt parched, and I was groggy from whatever drug Justin had injected me with. "We weren't sure if you'd wake up," a soft female voice said.

I focused on the voice, blinking to clear my vision. After a few seconds, I saw her face, lit by the glow of a battery-powered lamp. She was young, barely old enough to drink—just the kind of victim he preferred. "Do you have any water?" I managed to ask.

"Sure," she said. "Patty, could you hand me a bottle?" I couldn't see the other woman clearly, only her shadow as she handed over the bottle, unscrewing the lid for me.

"The drugs keep you weak for a few hours," the woman said, watching me with concern. "I'm Kendra, and that's Patty."

After a few long sips, I felt a bit stronger. "Thank you," I said. "Where are we?"

Patty's voice came from the shadows with a nervous

laugh. "Wish I knew."

Kendra explained, "We were both drugged and woke up here, in this metal storage container. You were dumped here last night by a man. Patty thought she recognized his voice, maybe someone she met at a bar, but I didn't know him. Do you remember what happened to you?"

I took another sip, weighing my words. They deserved the truth. "I was abducted by the killer they call the twenty-nine-day killer, or the full moon slayer."

Patty broke the silence first. "How do you know it was him? No one even knows who he is."

I nodded grimly. "Actually, I do. I've been tracking him for years, and I recently found out his real name and where he lives."

Kendra's eyes widened. "Then the police are closing in on him, right? You're a cop, aren't you?"

"No," I admitted. "I'm a private investigator. I'm sure the police know who he is by now, but I'm afraid they won't find us before the full moon rises."

Patty's voice trembled. "That's in just a couple of hours."

Kendra pulled her knees to her chest, rocking slightly. "Is he going to…do to us what he did to all those others? I can't die like this. I have people waiting for me."

Patty was pacing now, the confined space of the storage container making her movements frantic.

"Listen to me," I said, raising my voice. "We can survive this."

Patty stopped pacing, looking at me with desperation. "How?"

"He's one man, and there are three of us. If we stay calm, work together, and don't panic, we have a chance to take him down."

Kendra, still rocking, whispered, "I heard he's…not even human. Like some kind of skinwalker."

I moved to Kendra's side, placing a steadying hand on her arm. "I promise you, he's human. Flesh and blood, just like us. And he has weaknesses. I can teach you how to fight back."

They both nodded, fear mingling with newfound determination.

For the next two hours, I taught them every survival trick I knew—how to go for vulnerable spots, how to claw and strike when cornered. When the time came, I was confident that we'd make him regret underestimating us.

A loud buzzing sound filled the container, and the door popped open slightly. I realized Justin must have rigged an automatic release—he'd want his "prey" to have a head start for his twisted game. I led Kendra and Patty outside, into the cold, dark woods, the faint moonlight casting eerie shadows everywhere.

I spotted tire tracks leading from the container, forming a path through the trees. "If we follow these tracks, we'll find the road."

"That's the way he'll be coming," Patty protested.

"Maybe, but wandering aimlessly in the woods is even riskier," I replied.

Kendra shivered. "Why don't we ambush him here? It's three against one."

"Good idea," Patty agreed. "We'll use the element of surprise."

A distant howl pierced the night, sending a chill through all of us. Was it real? Or another part of his sick game? "Whatever we're doing, let's decide fast," I said.

Patty handed us each a large branch. "I'll stay here in the container, make noise to lure him in," Kendra said. "You two can hide outside and attack when he's distracted."

The plan set, I crouched behind a nearby tree, my heart pounding. A few minutes later, I heard heavy footsteps approaching. The crunching of leaves and snapping of branches was unnervingly loud in the stillness.

I peered around the tree, catching a glimpse of something large and shadowy. Red eyes glinted back at me, and I felt a jolt of terror. It was as if I was staring into the eyes of something monstrous.

Kendra was making noise from inside the container, but instead of drawing it in, the figure moved toward Patty's hiding spot, sniffing the air. Then, in a horrifying instant, it charged, and I heard Patty scream.

Instinct took over, and I ran, the sounds of Patty's final scream echoing in my ears. I crashed through branches and bushes, feeling only the need to escape.

I burst into a field, moonlight illuminating a nearby barn on a hill. I sprinted toward it, throwing myself through the slightly open door and slamming it shut behind me. The barn was old, musty, and dimly lit by beams of moonlight streaming through holes in the roof.

A ladder led up to the loft, the only other place to go. Halfway up, the barn door shook under a powerful blow. I climbed faster, but the ladder snapped just as I reached the top, sending me tumbling back down.

I lay on the ground, gasping, as the shadow loomed over me, teeth bared, saliva dripping. I threw an arm up in a desperate attempt to protect my face, and pain ripped through my arm as it bit down.

My hand searched frantically in the hay, fingers wrapping around something solid. With all my strength, I drove it into the side of the creature's head. It let out a guttural growl, backing off just enough for me to stagger to my feet.

Realizing I'd grabbed a pitchfork, I swung it again and again, stabbing until the creature slumped, motionless. The rush of adrenaline faded, and I became dimly aware of another figure by the door, gun raised.

Still caught in the frenzy, I charged, thrusting the pitchfork into him. He stumbled backward into the moonlight, and I saw his face—it was Justin, wrapped in animal skins, blood smeared across his face.

With one last kick, I knocked him out and looked around for an escape. In the distance, I spotted a power line and followed it, stumbling toward a house at the end.

An older couple opened the door, and though I tried to speak, exhaustion finally claimed me, and everything faded to black.

Chapter 12

I woke up in a hospital room again. One of my hands was handcuffed to the bed railings and parts of my body were wrapped tightly in thick bandages. Recent past events felt sort of unreal to me, but the evidence at hand confirmed to me that I had just lived through another life and death event.

I should be excited and overcome with joy at the knowledge that I had put a stop to the twenty-nine-day killer. I had avenged my family and all those poor women he had killed. In the end, though, I just felt alone and cold at the prospect that everything I had done. Was going to lead me to a jail cell and a life without anyone to be in it.

"Hey, you're awake."

The voice startled me to my right-hand side. I hadn't even glanced over that way until now. And to my pleasant surprise, Dan was now standing by my side taking my free hand into his. "After I left you, I didn't think you would ever want to talk with me again."

"Why would you think a dumb thing like that? I told you that I would help you in capturing this killer. You should've trusted me, Jenifer."

"I know, I just didn't want to put your life in jeopardy.

Especially after the death of your aunt. I was trying to protect you."

"I understand that. Do you realize how many laws you broke in order to find him?"

I nodded my head, trying not to add up how many charges would be brought against me. I had a pretty good guess in mind.

Dan squeezed my hand. "I've secured a lawyer for you from a family I know and trust. They will probably be in later today or tomorrow to talk with you. As well as the FBI and the local police, they have many questions for you concerning recent events."

"I'm sure they do," I said. "In fact, I have a couple of questions of my own. If you can answer them for me?"

"I'll tell you whatever I know. Some of the local deputies and police have at least given me some information."

"Do they have the killer in custody?"

"Yes, it's been on the news, and you did a number on him."

"I did a number on his wolf as well."

"That thing was a monster in size," Dan said. "I was told that it was a rare wild breed from out of the European back countries like Romania."

"Makes sense," I said. "He watched his sister get eaten by a pack of wolves. Somewhere in his traumatized brain, he began crafting his delusion about being a werewolf."

"Hadn't heard that story, but then again, the media is keeping quiet about his family and his past. One thing about the case I'm still trying to comprehend is why is there such a gap from the time he attacked your family to the killings over the past year?"

"The family sent him to Mexico. I'm sure that is where he raised and trained his wolf and began to hone his killing technique. A police detective that kept me up to date on the case passed some information onto me about killings happening in Mexico and the myths that was being spread of a skinwalker killing people."

"So, he has been killing for a long time then. I had no idea."

"Only a very few did, now you know why I was so obsessed. The authorities were not doing enough. How many more bodies did there need to be before Justin was captured? I had to do something about it."

He leaned over so that we were face to face now. "That's what I love about you. You were thinking about others and the greater good where most of us only focus on ourselves and our own pleasures. I don't know what the future holds for us, but I'm telling you right now that I will be with you, no matter what."

Our lips met and we kissed long and lovingly. I felt at peace at last.

Chapter 13

I sat across from my lawyer in the small, windowless conference room. The overhead light cast a harsh glow, illuminating the stack of documents in front of me—evidence, police reports, and transcripts of interviews from the past few days. The manila folder sat like a weight on the table between me and my attorney, thick and unyielding, much like the walls I felt closing in around me.

Dan had left just a few minutes ago, his hand squeezing mine in silent support before the officers called my lawyer in. Now, with him gone, the reality of the situation sank deeper into my bones. I felt stripped, laid bare by the weight of my actions and the law's inevitable judgment.

My lawyer, a seasoned woman in her forties named Marcy Kane, leaned forward, adjusting her glasses. "Jenifer," she began, her voice steady, "I need you to understand that what you did, no matter how justified it may have felt, is going to carry consequences. Vigilantism, breaking and entering, assault... these aren't small charges."

I nodded, swallowing hard. "I didn't... I mean, I never intended for things to get so... out of control. But it felt like no one else was doing anything. The police, the FBI—

they were just spinning their wheels. And all the while, he kept killing."

Marcy looked at me for a long moment, a hint of sympathy in her eyes. "I understand. And in a way, so will a lot of people. Public opinion is likely to lean in your favor. People love a hero, even a flawed one. But the justice system… it doesn't always see things in shades of gray."

My hands clenched into fists. "How can they call it justice if they'd rather bury evidence in red tape than save lives? I've been chasing him for years. And every time I got close, there was some bureaucratic barrier, some rule that kept me from catching him. If I hadn't taken things into my own hands, he'd still be out there, killing innocent women."

"I know," Marcy said, her voice softening. "And that's something we'll use in your defense. But you need to be prepared for what's coming. They're going to question everything—your methods, your motives, even your mental state."

With my shoulders sagging, I looked down at my hands. There was a faint scar on my right wrist, a reminder of an earlier encounter with the killer. I traced it with my thumb, feeling the roughness beneath my touch. "Maybe they're right to question me," I whispered. "Sometimes… I wonder if I crossed a line, if I became more like him than I ever intended. My sister, my family—they wouldn't recognize the person I became."

Marcy leaned back, crossing her arms as she studied me. "The truth is, Jenifer, you went through unimaginable trauma. And the law might struggle to see it, but those of us on the outside can understand. You hunted him because you felt responsible, because you were the only one left to remember, to seek justice."

I nodded slowly, biting back the sting of tears. "But that doesn't excuse what I did. I've hurt people, crossed boundaries I never thought I would. I wanted justice, but in the end, I think I wanted revenge even more."

Marcy placed a hand on my arm, a brief touch that held weight. "Then tell that to them. When they bring you in front of the judge, when they question you, be honest. Don't paint yourself as a hero, because they'll see through it. But let them see the human being underneath it all—the woman who fought because she had no other choice, who wanted to protect others from a monster."

I took a deep, shaky breath. "You think they'll listen?"

Marcy gave a small, sad smile. "Maybe. People aren't as blind to suffering as you think. But whether they do or not, you have to face this. You've taken on so much alone, and now… now it's time to let go, to accept whatever comes next."

As Marcy gathered her papers, preparing for the upcoming hearing, I sat in silence, letting her words wash over me. Let go. I had held onto my hatred, my grief, my need for revenge, for so long it had become a part of me. But now, with the killer behind bars and justice, or whatever semblance of it I could grasp, within reach, I felt that familiar rage start to ebb. In its place, a quiet numbness settled, bittersweet and strangely comforting.

The door opened, and the officers stepped in to escort me to the courtroom. Marcy offered me a reassuring nod as I rose to my feet.

"Whatever happens," I said, my voice barely above a whisper, "I hope… I hope my sister can rest now. And maybe, one day, I can find a way to forgive myself."

Marcy gave my hand a final squeeze. "Maybe you will, Jenifer. Maybe you will."

Chapter 14

Two weeks later. The courtroom was silent as I took my seat beside my attorney, Marcy Kane. The room was full, each row of benches packed with onlookers and reporters who had come to witness the trial of a woman who had become both infamous and, to some, heroic. The air buzzed with tension, curiosity, and judgment, and I could feel it all pressing down on me, heavier than I'd imagined.

At the prosecutor's table, Assistant District Attorney Michael Burns reviewed his notes, his eyes flickering up to meet mine before he returned to his papers with a stern, disapproving expression. He was here to make the jury see me not as a hero, but as a lawbreaker who had taken justice into her own hands.

Judge Harriet Ellison, an imposing figure with silver hair and sharp eyes, called the court to order, her gavel falling with a resolute thud. "The court will now hear the closing arguments. ADA Burns, you may begin."

Burns stood, buttoning his jacket and approaching the jury with an air of measured confidence. He glanced around the courtroom before finally focusing on the twelve jurors seated to the side, each one watching him intently.

"Ladies and gentlemen of the jury," he began, his voice clear and steady. "We are here because the defendant, Jenifer Walker, chose to ignore the rule of law. We are here because she decided that her personal vendetta took precedence over the system that was created to protect each and every one of us. Yes, her story is tragic. Yes, she suffered a great loss, but that does not give her the right to take the law into her own hands."

He paused, his gaze unwavering. "She broke into homes, assaulted individuals, and in her obsession, she disregarded the boundaries set by our society. The defendant's actions led to pain and suffering for others, and her choice to act as judge, jury, and executioner undermines the very foundation of our justice system. If we allow people to act outside of the law, then we are opening a door to chaos—a door to a world where everyone makes their own rules, decides who deserves punishment, and acts on impulse rather than order."

Burns took a step closer to the jury. "No one is denying that Jenifer went through hell, but we cannot ignore the fact that she committed crimes—crimes that hurt others. Today, you must decide whether we are a nation of laws or a nation of vigilantes. I ask you to uphold the law and hold Ms. Walker accountable for her actions."

He nodded respectfully to the judge before returning to his seat, his gaze never leaving the jurors as he sat down. There was a palpable weight in the room as his words settled, and I could feel the tension tighten in my chest.

Judge Ellison looked to Marcy and nodded. "Ms. Kane, you may proceed."

Marcy rose, her expression calm yet resolute. She walked to the center of the courtroom, pausing to collect her thoughts before turning to face the jury, her eyes gentle and steady.

"Ladies and gentlemen, today you've heard a story about a woman who endured unimaginable loss. You've seen the evidence, you've heard the witnesses, and you know what Jenifer Walker went through. You know what it's like to feel powerless, to be a victim, and you understand how, sometimes, the systems meant to protect us can fail."

She glanced toward me, and I met her gaze briefly before looking down at my hands. "Jenifer was once a young woman with a family, with people she loved and a future ahead of her. That all changed in one night, when everything was stolen from her by a monster who would go on to terrorize countless others. She was the only one left to carry that burden, the only one left to remember and fight. And fight she did—not out of anger, but out of a desire for justice, a desire to protect others from the horror that she experienced."

Marcy took a step closer to the jury, her voice soft but filled with conviction. "Jenifer reached out to law enforcement, she reported her suspicions, and she followed every lead she had. And each time, she was met with walls, with red tape, with bureaucratic delays. The system she believed in left her alone to face the darkness. So she took matters into her own hands, not because she wanted to break the law, but because she felt she had no other choice."

Her gaze swept across the faces of the jurors, her expression one of quiet plea. "None of us can truly know what we would do in Jenifer's place. We sit here, in the safety of this courtroom, far removed from the terror and the grief she endured. But imagine, just for a moment, the desperation that would drive someone to act as she did. Imagine the pain and frustration of watching the man who destroyed your life walk free, of knowing he would hurt others. Wouldn't you feel compelled to act?"

Marcy paused, letting the question linger in the air. "Jenifer Walker is not a criminal. She is a survivor. She is a woman who fought to make sure no one else would have to live through the nightmare she endured. Yes, she made mistakes. Yes, she crossed lines. But her actions came from a place of courage, from a heart that refused to let evil go unanswered."

She took a breath, her voice lowering. "So today, I ask you to consider her humanity. I ask you to consider her suffering, her loss, and her sacrifice. I ask you to show mercy to a woman who has already endured more than most of us could imagine. I ask you to see her not as a vigilante, but as a person who sought justice when the system failed her."

Marcy looked at the jury, a final plea in her eyes. "Please, do not punish her for wanting to make the world a safer place. She has paid a price greater than any sentence could impose. I ask you to find her not guilty, and to give her a chance to find peace."

She nodded to the judge and returned to her seat, placing a comforting hand on my shoulder. Judge Ellison turned to the jury, her face solemn.

"Members of the jury," she said, her voice carrying a weight that settled over the room, "you have heard the arguments from both sides. It is now your responsibility to deliberate and reach a verdict. The decision lies in your hands."

With a final strike of her gavel, she dismissed the jury to begin their deliberations. I closed my eyes, feeling the enormity of the moment. My fate was now out of my control, held in the hands of twelve strangers who would determine whether I walked free or paid for the choices I had made in my pursuit of justice.

Chapter 15

I sat on the cold, hard bench of the courthouse holding cell, my fingers nervously tracing patterns on the concrete wall beside me. The faint buzz of the fluorescent lights above felt oppressive, matching the weight of uncertainty pressing on my chest. I tried to keep my thoughts steady, but each passing minute brought me closer to a future I couldn't control.

The metallic clang of the door interrupted my thoughts. My lawyer, Marcy Kane stepped inside, a small smile on her face as she set a folder on the bench. "Jenifer," she began, her voice calm and steady, "I wanted to come by and give you an update."

I straightened up, searching Marcy's eyes for any hint of news. Marcy sat beside me, taking a moment before speaking. "They've decided that Justin Tompkins will be tried in North Carolina. Given the charges, they're going for the death penalty."

For a second, I felt a numbness wash over me. Justin's trial, his potential death sentence—it felt surreal. I knew I should feel a sense of victory, but my emotions were tangled, a mix of relief, anger, and exhaustion. "So he'll pay for what he did," I whispered, my voice barely audible.

"Yes," Marcy replied gently. "Justice will be served. But right now, we're focused on you." She reached into her folder and pulled out a neatly folded envelope. "And… there's something else. Dan wanted me to pass this to you. He hasn't been able to visit, but he thought this might help."

My fingers trembled slightly as I took the letter, carefully opening it. Dan's familiar handwriting greeted me, and as I began to read, the world around me seemed to soften.

"Jenifer," the letter began, "I know you're probably feeling lost, but I need you to know how much I believe in you. You did what others wouldn't—what others couldn't—and that's something that takes courage beyond measure. You were fighting for justice, for closure, and no matter what happens in that courtroom, I want you to know that you're not alone. I'm here, waiting for you, believing in you."

I swallowed hard, feeling a lump in my throat as I continued reading.

"I can't imagine the weight you've been carrying all these years. But you've made it this far, and I know you'll make it through this too. You have a future, Jenifer. And I'm hoping I can be a part of it. Just hold on a little longer. The jury will see what I see—a woman who deserves a chance, who deserves freedom."

The words wrapped around me like a warm embrace, giving me a glimmer of hope and strength I hadn't felt in days. Dan's unwavering belief in me was a balm for my weary heart, a reminder that someone outside this sterile courtroom and this cold cell understood me. Someone still cared.

Marcy waited, giving me a moment to collect myself. Then, as if sensing the perfect moment, her phone buzzed with a message. She glanced down and looked back up, meeting my gaze.

"The jury has reached a decision," Marcy said softly, her tone a mixture of seriousness and encouragement. "It's time."

I took a deep breath, folding Dan's letter carefully and placing it back in the envelope, holding it close. Marcy gave me a reassuring nod, and together, we rose from the bench and walked through the silent hallways toward the courtroom.

The walk felt surreal, each step echoing louder than the last. When I entered the courtroom, I felt every eye turn to me, and I steadied myself, gripping the edge of the table as I sat down beside my lawyer. Marcy leaned in, giving me a small, supportive smile before settling in herself.

The judge addressed the jury foreman, a woman in her early forties who looked both solemn and resolute as she held the verdict slip in her hands. The entire room held its breath, each second stretching into an eternity.

The foreman cleared her throat, her voice steady as she read aloud. "We, the jury, find the defendant guilty on all charges, with a recommendation for a reduced sentence."

I felt a wave of emotions—relief, gratitude, exhaustion, and a bittersweet sense of closure. I glanced at Marcy, who gave me an encouraging nod, and then her eyes scanned the room, as if hoping that somehow, through all the faces, Dan might be watching.

The judge turned to the jury, thanking them for their service and formally accepting their recommendation. He then addressed me directly. "Ms. Walker, the court recognizes the unique nature of your case and the circumstances surrounding your actions. You will be given an opportunity for redemption and rehabilitation, in light of the jury's recommendation. You will serve two years in jail and one year in community service. All while participating in counseling."

As the judge concluded, I felt the weight of years of pain and vengeance lift, just a little. I closed my eyes, Dan's letter clutched tightly in my hand, knowing that, at last, my journey toward justice—and maybe even peace—was beginning anew.

Chapter 16

The familiar clang and buzz of the prison doors echoed through the visiting area, and my heart pounded harder with each step. I knew Dan was just on the other side, waiting for me, and as I spotted him across the room, my heart surged with a mix of joy and relief. He looked different somehow—more solid, more real. I hadn't realized how much I'd missed him until he was right there, standing in front of me, reaching for my hands.

"Jen," he said softly, his voice filled with warmth. He pulled me into a brief, fierce hug, and I closed my eyes, savoring the rare feeling of closeness. In this place, small gestures like this meant everything.

"Dan," I whispered back as we took our seats. "It's so good to see you."

He gave me a smile that melted away the weeks of stress and fear. "It's good to see you too, Jen. How are you holding up?"

I took a deep breath, gathering my thoughts. "Actually, I have some news," I said, trying to keep my voice steady, though excitement bubbled underneath. "The parole board… they're meeting in a couple of weeks to review my case. There's a chance I might get out early."

His face broke into that huge, beautiful grin of his. "Jen, that's… that's incredible! Really?" He squeezed my hands, and I felt the genuine joy radiating from him.

I nodded, feeling hope build within me, like a light breaking through the darkness. "It's not certain yet, but yes. There's a real chance, Dan. I can hardly believe it."

"You deserve this, Jen," he said, his voice filled with certainty. "After everything you've been through, this is finally something good."

He was right, but I could barely wrap my head around it. I'd spent so long here, imagining this moment but never daring to hope too much. Before I could sink too deeply into my thoughts, Dan continued.

"There's more," he said, a little more serious now. "I wanted to tell you about… Justin. The case, it's over. He was convicted on all charges. They sentenced him to death. He's waiting for lethal injection."

For a moment, I closed my eyes, letting the words settle. After all the pain, all the years of searching, of fighting—finally, there was justice. A wave of bittersweet relief washed over me. "Thank you, Dan. For staying with me through all of this. I don't know what I would've done without you."

"You don't have to thank me," he said, brushing his thumb across my knuckles. "I'd do it all again for you." He hesitated, looking down at our hands for a moment before he spoke again. "There's something else I wanted to ask you."

I raised an eyebrow, curious. "What is it?"

"Aunt Beth's house—it's mine now. I've been fixing it up, making it feel like home." He took a breath, looking suddenly vulnerable. "When you get out... would you want to live there with me?"

My heart skipped a beat, and I felt tears prick at the corners of my eyes. After everything, the idea of living with Dan, of having a real home to go to... it felt like a dream I hadn't let myself believe was possible. I squeezed his hands, nodding. "I'd love that, Dan. More than anything."

We shared a quiet moment, leaning forward until our foreheads touched, just taking in the feeling of finally having something to look forward to. In the dim, clinical lighting of the prison visiting room, it felt like the most beautiful place in the world.

Before I knew it, a guard was clearing his throat, signaling that time was up. Dan and I exchanged a final hug, clinging to each other as long as we could. When he pulled back, he gave me one last reassuring smile before he walked away, and I watched him go, holding onto the warmth of his presence like a lifeline.

***

The next few weeks felt like an eternity. The days dragged, but finally, the day came for my parole hearing. I sat in front of the board, trying to keep my head held high, reminding myself of all I'd been through, of how far I'd come. I answered their questions as best as I could, my voice steady, though my heart raced with every word.

They deliberated while I waited, my hands folded tightly in my lap. Every minute felt like an hour, my mind racing through every possible outcome. Finally, they called me back in, and one of the board members looked at me, his expression warm.

"Ms. Walker, after careful consideration, we've decided that you've served your time. You're granted parole."

A rush of relief flooded through me, so intense I thought I might break down right there. I managed to nod, blinking back tears. "Thank you," I whispered, hardly able to believe it.

***

The day I was released was bright and warm, the sun beaming down as I stepped out of the gates. And there, leaning against his car with that same, familiar grin, was Dan. As soon as he saw me, he broke into a run, sweeping me up in a hug that made me feel, for the first time in years, truly free.

"Welcome home, Jen," he whispered in my ear, his voice thick with emotion.

We didn't need to say much on the drive. I soaked in the world outside the window, the sky, the trees, the open road—all of it felt new and alive. And then, finally, we pulled up to Aunt Beth's house. It looked fresh, vibrant, as though it were waiting for us to fill it with life.

As we walked inside, Dan took my hand, leading me through the rooms he'd carefully restored. I felt a surge of gratitude, of love, and a deep, overwhelming sense of peace. This was our place, our beginning, a chance to start over together.

And for the first time in so many years, I felt like I was home.

Epilogue

I sat in the quiet, dimly lit viewing room, surrounded by a handful of others, each person carrying their own reasons, their own burdens. I felt a deep stillness within me, a contrast to the storm of emotions I'd endured over the past years. I was no stranger to loss or pain, but this moment felt different—a culmination, a final chapter in the dark story that had defined so much of my life.

Through the glass, I watched as Justin Tompkins was led into the sterile chamber, his wrists shackled, his steps heavy. He wore a look of defiance, a sneer that spoke to the years of terror he'd inflicted. But I saw something else in his eyes, too—fear. A primal, unmistakable fear of what was coming, a fear that no amount of rage or cruelty could disguise.

At first, Justin resisted, pulling against the guards as they guided him toward the gurney. His defiance flared, his body struggling in a last attempt to assert control, but the guards remained calm, professional, and firm. Slowly, they subdued him, securing his arms and legs with leather straps, pinning him down in a way that left him completely vulnerable, completely powerless. The contrast between this moment and the memory of his monstrous acts was striking, almost surreal.

My hand instinctively went to my stomach, my fingers pressing gently against the small but undeniable curve. A sense of calm washed over me, grounding me as I witnessed the final moments of the man who had taken so much from me and my family. But he hadn't taken everything. Life had continued; a new life was growing, and the thought brought me a quiet sense of resilience.

The guard's voice cut through the silence, asking Justin if he had any final words. For a moment, Justin just stared at the ceiling, a look of hollow fury in his eyes. Then he turned his gaze toward the glass, his voice dripping with bitterness.

"You think this changes anything? You think you've won?" he spat, his voice sharp and acidic. "I'll haunt you forever. This isn't the end—it's just the beginning."

The words hung heavy in the air, echoing in the silent chamber. I held his gaze, feeling nothing but a quiet resolve as he spoke. His power over me was gone; I knew that now. His threats meant nothing.

A nod from the warden, and the execution team began the process, inserting the IVs into Justin's arm, preparing the solution that would end his life. As the drugs were administered, Justin's expression softened, his anger fading, his face paling as the sedative took hold. His breathing slowed, his eyes grew unfocused, and eventually, his head lolled back, the defiance and malice slipping away.

My hand remained on my stomach, rubbing gently, feeling the faintest flutter beneath my palm—a small reminder of the life I carried. I breathed deeply, feeling the weight of my past lift, as if Justin's passing had finally severed the last tether that held me to the trauma he had caused. I wasn't alone in the world, not anymore. I had Dan, and soon, a new beginning.

The warden announced the time of death, marking the end of Justin Tompkins. But for me, it wasn't just his end—it was my freedom, a release from the shadows that had haunted me for so long.

As I left the room, I whispered quietly to myself, "It's over."